C000246406

THE UNEXPURGATED ADVENTURES OF

SHERLOCK HOLMES

BOOK 3

THE CASE OF THE
RANDY STEPFATHER

by NP Sercombe

The un-edited manuscript originally entitled
The Case of Identity written by
Dr. John Watson and Sir Arthur Conan Doyle

Illustrations by Emily Snape

Published by EVA BOOKS 2019 – c/o Harry King Films Limited
1&2 The Barn
West Stoke Road
Lavant
n/r Chichester
West Sussex PO18 9AA

A CIP catalogue record for this book is available from the British Library.

ISBN 978-1-9996961-2-2 (Hardback)

Book layout & Cover design by Clare Brayshaw.

Cover illustration by Emily Snape.

Set in Bruce Old Style.

Prepared and printed by: York Publishing Services Ltd
64 Hallfield Road, Layerthorpe, York YO31 7ZQ

Tel: 01904 431213

Website: www.yps-publishing.co.uk

THE UNEXPURGATED ADVENTURES OF

SHERLOCK HOLMES

Books in the Series:

Nicholas Sercombe is a writer and producer for film and television. He has been lucky enough to work in comedy for most of the Holocene period with some of the greatest performers and writers. He is most comfortable when reading Conan Doyle and even happier when re-writing these extraordinarily entertaining stories by Dr. John Watson.

Emily Snape is a coffee addicted, London based illustrator, who's work can be found internationally on books, magazines, the web, television and even on buses.

She studied at Central Saint Martins, Bristol and Kingston and is rarely found without a pencil in her hand. She loves sketching in the streets of London and thinks life is too short for matching socks.

For generously-proportioned people who enjoy laughing

The Case of the Randy Stepfather

(*published in The Strand in September 1891 as*
A CASE OF MISTAKEN IDENTITY by
Dr. Watson and Arthur Conan Doyle)

' **M**y dear fellow,' said Sherlock Holmes, as we sat one morning on either side of the fire in our lodgings at Baker Street, 'what of this affair with your nephew and your new patients?'

'I'd prefer not to debate the moral failings of young Will,' I said to Holmes. 'His intentions were admirable, but I would have ended up being struck off.' It turned out that young Will, who I had hired recently to be my new practice secretary, had recruited into my patient register a number of war veterans from the army who expected me to write scripts for powerful narcotics to allay their terrible nightmares; their legacies from fighting for Queen and country. I wanted to help those poor souls but doling out cocaine and morphine willy-nilly would, of course, kill them slowly at arm's length. I would not do that. Besides, I was a private doctor in an expensive practice – how could I charge them for my services?

'Young William may have been entrepreneurial,' I said, 'but he recruited under an untested incentive and made unwise selections.'

'You will have to let him go, I presume?'

'No, I cannot do that Holmes. His family is desperately short of relatives. He attends to his sick mother on his own. I see a boy with good heart. I have given him a second chance, in the hope that he may harvest a more bountiful crop.'

'You sent him back to the veterans to purchase you an army revolver.'

'Holmes! How on Earth did you know that?!'

'The painted water pistol you waved at John Clay in the bank vault wouldn't fool a fly.'*

'By Jingo, Holmes, you noticed that? Why didn't you say something?'

'He believed it to be the real thing.'

'So did that policeman.'

'Yes, but Inspector Jones is only a police detective.'

'And he was Welsh...'

'It was Clay who went down in my estimation. There is a villain who should know a real gun when he sees one! I suppose life is infinitely stranger than anything which the mind of man could invent,' said Holmes philosophically. 'We would not dare conceive the things which are really mere commonplace of existence, your nephew's procurements being a prime example of what lies beneath the commonality. If we could fly out of that window hand in hand, hover over this great city, gently remove the roofs, and peep in at the queer things which are going on...'

'We would be arrested as peeping toms and locked up within minutes,' I quipped, trying to lighten the atmosphere a little.

---

* see *The Mysterious Case of Mr. Gingernuts*

'Do not interrupt my musing, Doctor,' he snapped, and then continued unabated, 'the strange coincidences, the plannings, the cross-purposes, the wonderful chain of events, working through the generations, and leading to the most *outré* results, it would make all the fiction with its confrontational and foreseen conclusions most stale and unprofitable.'

'And yet I am not convinced of it,' I mused back to him. 'The cases which come to light in the papers are, as a rule, bald enough, and vulgar enough. We have in our police reports realism pushed to its extreme limits, and yet the result is, it must be confessed, neither fascinating nor artistic.'

'Police reports? My word, you are on the right scent, Watson!' remarked Holmes. 'A certain selection and discretion must be used in producing a realistic effect. This is wanting in the police report, where more stress is laid perhaps upon the platitudes of the magistrate than upon the details, which to an observer contain the vital essence of the whole matter. Depend upon it there is nothing so unnatural as the commonplace.'

I smiled and shook my head. 'I can quite understand you thinking so,' I said. 'Of course, in your position of unofficial adviser and helper to everybody, who is absolutely puzzled, throughout three continents, you are brought in to contact with all that is strange and bizarre. But here' – I picked up the morning paper from the floor – 'let us put it to a practical test. Here is the first heading upon which I come. "A husband's cruelty to his wife." There is half a column of print, but I know, without even reading it, that it is all perfectly familiar to me. There is, of course: the other woman, the drink, the push, the blow, the bruise, the sympathetic sister or landlady. The crudest writers could invent nothing cruder.'

'Indeed? Well, your example is an unfortunate one for your argument,' said Holmes, taking the paper, and glancing his eye down it. 'This is the Dundas separation case, and, as it happens, I was engaged in clearing up some small points in connection with it.'

I sank into my armchair, like a burst balloon. I closed my eyes and counted to five. How did he do it? The one, single story I had picked out for use as an example, the first one that my eye rested upon, and Holmes just had to be involved in it, didn't he? It would not have made any difference if I had selected any of the other headlines, such as "Cat stuck up tree," or "Pope appears on balcony," he would pipe up: "Oh yes, I was engaged in clearing up some small points... Oh I had a hand in bringing that to a successful conclusion." It never ended! One case after another, most of which he didn't even tell me about.

'You see, Watson, you were so wrong. Look here... The husband was a teetotaler, there was no other woman, and the conduct complained of was that he had drifted into the habit of winding up every meal by taking out his false teeth and hurling them at his wife, which you will allow is not an action likely to occur to the imagination of the average story-teller. Take a pinch of snuff, Doctor, and acknowledge that I have scored over you in your example.'

There he was, holding out his snuffbox of old gold, with a great amethyst in the centre of the lid, and the inside full of fine, white powder.

'My dear friend, you have taken far too much of that "snuff" if you think I am going to believe that!'

'This particular variety lightens your perspective upon the grievances of the day, given five minutes or so. Here, grab a Robin's egg of the good life!'

I shook my head. Holmes plunged his thumb and forefingers into the casket to pinch a healthy amount of the powder, probably about the size of a small bird's egg, and, in a single movement, whisked it skillfully up each nostril.

'Then, pray, read the article good Doctor.' And he chucked the paper back to me. I wrestled the sheets back into some sort of order and flicked my eye across the text of the article in question. Sadly enough, the dispute was all about the dentures, just as the great detective had described. And there, in the final paragraph, was the name S.N.J. Holmes Esq. I looked up to see the gold snuff casket under my nose again. Its splendour was in such contrast to his homely ways and simple life that I could not help commenting upon it.

'No thanks, Holmes. Why, that is a rather a superb casket. Where did you get it from?'

'Ah,' said he, 'I forgot that I had not mentioned to you before. It is a little souvenir from the King of Bohemia in return for my assistance in the case of the Irene Adler papers.'

A bolt of electricity shot through my body!

'The King of Bohemia gave you that?!' I cried.

'Hmm, yes? He was most gracious... as most kings and queens are. You seem surprised, Watson. Why would that be?'

You may remember, dear adventure-enthusiast, that in my previous account, *A Balls-Up in Bohemia*, Sherlock Holmes had thrown a fit of *pique* when Irene Adler avoided his trap and escaped with a compromising photograph she had of the King of Bohemia (the "papers" that he had just claimed to have recovered). As the thwarted detective stomped off towards Baker Street in a bate, the King and I had come to a financial arrangement that had paid for our services. Nothing unreasonable in that, of course, until I used the five thousand to settle my divorce with Mary Morstan whilst Holmes was still under the impression that Mary and I had settled our differences for forty pounds. You can see now why I might be alarmed at their consequent communication!

'You met with the King after our last encounter with him at Briony Lodge?' I asked, in great trepidation of the answer.

'Oh no. It was dropped into the apartment by one of his flunkeys. Curiously, there was a card accompanying it which read: "Money is not everything." I related that to the seven hundred pounds he had advanced me for expenses. He had not requested their return.'

'A brilliant deduction, Holmes!'

Phew!

'Remarkable, Holmes, remarkable!' I enthused. The great detective inclined his head at my effusiveness, with a slightly suspicious look in his eye, so I decided it was time to get him off the subject. 'I say, Holmes, what is that ring upon your finger? Have you turned Romany?'

'Oh, ha ha, Watson! You could not be further from the truth. This ring was a gift from the reigning family of Holland, though the matter in which I served them was of such delicacy that I cannot confide it even to you, who have been good enough to chronicle one or two of my little problems.'

'I rather wish I had been privy to the case of such delicacy in Dutchland, Holmes. It sounds quite alluring.'

'It was gruesome and sordid, my friend, and certainly a story best forgotten and certainly never to be chronicled.'

I licked my lips in anticipation; this had the potential to be a five-star story! 'Perish the thought, Holmes. But you can tell me what happened. Come on! We are the very best of friends and you know that I am the very soul of discretion.'

'My dear Doctor, you would not be interested in a mystery that involved a goose, a horse's bridle, a small pen-knife, a Toulouse salami, an intimate tattooist, a velvet cord, a hypodermic needle and a Van der Graff generator. So, that's an end to it.'

He had risen from his chair, and was standing between the parted blinds, gazing down into the dull, neutral-tinted London street. I stood up, grasping the gold casket *en route*. I looked over his shoulder. I saw that on the pavement opposite there stood a very large woman with a heavy fur boa around her neck, and a large curling red feather in a broad-brimmed hat which was tilted in coquettish, Duchess of Devonshire fashion, over her ear.

'How about some Dutch courage, Holmes?' I swung my arm around him, placing the casket under his nose.

'Try as you may, Doctor, you will not loosen my tongue. My constitution is well-acquainted with its dreamy side-effects.' He pinched a small *soupçon* – a Wren's egg? – and then pushed it away, but without taking his eyes off the colossus outside.

'Dammit! Tell me, Holmes, what is it about that great big fat woman over there that holds such an interest for you? She is hardly your style.'

'That is a very personal opinion, Doctor. That great big fat woman over there may not have any choice about being so large. Maybe she has a glandular failure? And what, for instance, would be the difference if she was suffering a medical condition that is affecting her size?'

'Pah! A one in a million chance, Holmes. See how her fat wobbles! She eats too much. And I'll wager she complains about side-effects, like sciatica, as if they were stand-alone illnesses.'

'Sciatica, really?'

'An age-old excuse for fatties, Holmes.'

'Hmm... Look at her again, Watson. Ignore her size. Observe her mannerisms! She is nervous, hesitating fashion at our windows, oscillating backwards and forwards, and her fingers are fidgeting with her glove buttons. I have seen those symptoms before. She is about to do something with us. And look! There she goes!'

Suddenly, with a plunge, as of a diver who leaves the board, she hurried across the road.

I shouted "WIDE LOAD!" but, strangely, Holmes did not find my quip amusing.

'Look, Holmes!' I cried. 'Doesn't she remind you of a hippopotamus leaving the riverbank?'

But my friend didn't rise. He did not even smile, which was very strange. Normally, we shared the same vein of humour when it came to commenting upon the more extraordinary human beings of everyday life, but not this time. In fact, he turned away from the window altogether emitting a rather gruff cough. I only had time to shout out "wide load!" before we heard the sharp clang of the front doorbell.

'Watson! Quickly now! We must find a chair that will accommodate this lady without causing her embarrassment.'

We sprang into action, scanning our own furniture for a suitable chair, but to no avail.

'There is none nearly large enough, Holmes!'

'This is desperate, Doctor!' Holmes rushed over to his bedroom door and peered into the room. Nothing suitable resided in there. Next, he tried my bedroom and, suddenly, he became inspired. 'Watson! If we were to remove the side cushions from the Mummy Couch that you have in here, it will suffice!'

The chair Holmes had selected was an Egyptian Revival couch; a tall, single seat upright designed for the placing of an unconscious human body in such position that it could not fall backwards or from the sides. It was a metal frame construction, and therefore adequately substantial not to fall over under stress. When it was given to me by my dear grandmother, I was told that maybe it was designed as an embalming chair by the Egyptians. It was an ideal parking bay for the large lady that we had in mind.

He ran back over the to the fireplace and made room beside our chairs. I asked him: 'by "we", do you mean "me?"'

'Yes. Carry it over here and place it by the fire. Quickly now!'

Dear Lord! As I braced myself and lifted the hundredweight of furniture, I was the captive audience he required to deliver another deduction.

'Whilst you do that, consider this,' he said. 'That oscillation upon the pavement always means an *affaire du cœur*. The lady would like advice, but is not sure that the matter is not too delicate for communication. And yet even here we may discriminate. When a woman has been seriously wronged by a man she no longer oscillates, and the usual symptom is a broken bell wire.' Holmes cocked an ear as the door bell was pulled strongly again. I nodded in appreciation as I trotted over to my bedroom holding the cushions stacked high and threw them in.

Holmes continued. 'Here we may take it that there is a love matter, but that the maiden is not so much angry as perplexed, or grieved. But here she comes in person to resolve our doubts.'

As he spoke there was a tap at the door, and Mrs. Hudson entered to announce Miss Mary Sutherland, while the lady herself loomed behind her small figure like a full-sailed galleon behind a tiny pilot boat. Sherlock Holmes welcomed her with the easy courtesy for which he was remarkable, and having closed the door, he bowed her into the armchair that we had prepared. He looked over her in the minute it took to dock her stern into the space. The chair's frame creaked ominously! Holmes and I exchanged nervous glances. But she made it. Once she had wriggled herself into comfort, he delivered a greeting of the most abstract fashion, which was peculiar to him, and it helped to ease the tension in the room.

'Do you not find,' he said, 'that with your short sight and gigantic bosom it is a little trying to do so much typewriting?'

'I did at first,' she answered, 'but now I know where the letters are without looking.' Then, suddenly realising the full purport of his words, she gave a violent start, and looked up with fear and astonishment upon her broad, good-humored face. 'You cheeky scamp! You've heard about me before, Mr. Holmes,' she cried, 'or how else how could you know all that, and even the size of my bust?'

'Never mind,' said Holmes, laughing, 'it is my business to know things. Perhaps I have trained myself to see what others overlook. If not, why should you come to consult me?' Holmes took his seat again by the fire.

'I came to see you, sir, because I heard of you from Mrs. Etherege, whose husband you found so easy when the police and everyone had given him up for dead. Oh, Mr. Holmes, I wish you would do as much for me. I'm not rich, but still I have a hundred a year in my own right, besides the little that I make by the machine, and I would give it all to know what has become of Mr. Hosmer Angel.'

Here we go again! Yet another enquiry from the Jewish community. Just how they managed to attract trouble in such vast quantity one could not possibly imagine, but they all seemed to end up here, in Baker Street, with amazing frequency. Maybe Jewish people thought that the name Sherlock was Jewish? Come to think of it, *was* it Jewish? Was *he* Jewish? Hmmm!

'Why did you come away to consult me in a such a hurry?' asked Sherlock, with his fingertips together, and his eyes to the ceiling.

Again, a startled look came over the somewhat vacuous face of Miss Mary Sutherland. 'Yes, I did rush out of the house,' she said, 'for it made me angry to see the easy way in which Mr. Windibank – that is my Father – took it all. He would not go to the police, and he would not go to you, and so at last, as he would do nothing, and kept on saying that there was no harm done, it made me mad, and I just threw on my things and came right away to you.'

'Your Father?' said Holmes. 'Your Stepfather, surely, since the name is different?'

'Yes, my stepfather. I call him father, though it sounds funny, too, for he is only five years and two months older than myself.'

'And your Mother is alive?'

'Oh yes, Mother is alive and well, thank you. I wasn't best pleased, Mr. Holmes, when she married again so soon after Father's death, and a man who was nearly fifteen years younger than herself. Father was a plumber in the Tottenham Court Road, and he left a tidy business behind him, which Mother carried on with Mr. Hardy, the Foreman, but when Mr. Windibank came he made her sell the business, for he was very superior, being a traveller in wines. They got four thousand seven hundred for the goodwill and interest, which wasn't near as much as father could have got if he had been alive.'

I glanced over to Sherlock Holmes. After this long-winded rambling of complete banality, I had expected to see him impatient or asleep, but on the contrary, the snuff was having its evil way with him, and he had listened with the greatest concentration of attention.

'Your own little income,' he asked, 'does it come out of the business?'

'Oh, no, sir, it is quite separate, and what was left me by my Uncle Ned in Auckland. It is in New Zealand stock...'

Sheep!

'...and paying four and a half per cent.'

Not sheep...

'Two thousand five hundred pounds was the amount, but I can only touch the interest.'

'You *interest* me extremely,' joked Holmes. 'And since you draw so large a sum as a hundred a year, with what you earn into the bargain, you no doubt travel a little and indulge yourself in every way. I believe that a single lady can get on very nicely upon an income of about sixty pounds.'

'I could so with much less than that, Mr. Holmes, but you understand that as long as I live at home I don't wish to be a burden on them, and so they have the use of the money just while I am staying with them. Of course, that is only just for the time. Mr. Windibank draws my interest every quarter, and pays it over to Mother, and I find that I can do pretty well with what I earn at typewriting. It brings me twopence a sheet, and I can often do from fifteen to twenty sheets a day.'

BORING! Now we had to suffer the details about her cost of living! I threw another glance at Holmes, my eyes launching distress flares, which he caught sight of. He jumped up out of his chair. He turned to face me, with dramatic speed, his face a picture of devilment and a twisted lip for full effect.

'Tell me, Doctor, as you seem to be in touch with the market rates of typing pool labour more than I, would you say that twopence a sheet is reasonable? Or is poor Miss Sutherland here being under-paid and taken advantage of?'

'Thank you, Holmes,' I answered. Then, I understood that silly look on his face and decided that he was playing a trick upon me, trying to provoke a moment of extreme silliness at the expense of this rather tedious person and her rather trivial problem. I stared straight into his smirking eye and acknowledged the challenge.

'Yes, Holmes. By good fortune and natural coincidence, it was only yesterday that I was reading up on the current reckonings.'

'Ah! What a fine coincidence! Where would that have been, Doctor? In the *Typist Gazette*?'

'Hmm! An interesting publication, Holmes, but no. In fact, I haven't come across that title...'

'Surely you have?'

'No, surely I have not. It was written in *Secretarial & Admin Monthly*.'

Holmes stifled a laugh. 'Really? Ha, ha! Very, very good, Doctor!' And, then, he couldn't hold it in any longer, the snuff acting as the catalyst to our mischievous humour. He bent over, laughing heartily, slapping his thigh, and hissing 'Yes, yes, of course! *Secretarial Monthly*!'

'*Secretarial AND Admin Monthly*, Holmes.'

'Ha, ha, ha! *So* sorry! *My* mistake!' And he slapped his thigh some more.

'What *is* so funny, Mr. Holmes?' enquired our alarmed guest. But Holmes could not answer her for now he could not stop himself from laughing. So, I took my opportunity to turn the screw. I turned to face the large woman and stared at her with unwavering solemnity.

'You see, Miss Sutherland, you may think, and, indeed, you may have heard, that I am a Doctor of Medicine. But I am, in fact... a Doctor of Typing.'

That did it! Holmes collapsed onto the floor, holding his midriff, with tears were rolling out of his eyes and onto the Azerbaijani prayer mat. Now, Miss Sutherland became suspicious that something was wrong.

'Is that so?' she said, her voice laced with cynicism. 'Well I ain't never heard of such a publication! You are sure that you know what you are talking about, Doctor?'

'Oh yes, I do, indeed! That is why I know that these typing rates, per sheet, were also debated at the recent, annual... global... gathering of other doctors of typing.' I rummaged through the left side of my brain for a creative name… 'The infamous *Ribbons and Spools Conference!*'

Holmes went into yet another fit of laughter and shouted: 'The one in Davos?'

'No. In Zermatt.' I replied.

He rolled around laughing even more. But now I was beginning to become infected; I cracked a minuscule smile across my poker face, which was noticed by our guest.

'I think that you are taking advantage of my situation!' exclaimed Miss Sutherland, trying to sound angry and waving her finger at me, and then at Holmes (luckily, she didn't try to stand up to strengthen her scolding or she would have taken the Mummy Couch with her).

'Perish the thought, dear lady!' I assured her. She didn't know what to do next, or what to say. She sat still, drumming her pudgy fingers upon her fleshy thighs. As Holmes pull himself together and started to calm down, I thought that I would try to steer the mood back to sensibility.

'Please excuse us and let me explain. Before your arrival today, which was unforeseen, I had prescribed Mr. Holmes some medication that made him light-headed. Now, I think you have made your position very clear to us, Miss Sutherland. My friend, Mr. Shy…Mr. Sherlock Holmes is an expert on just about any subject you care to consult him upon. I see that he has made a complete recovery, kindly tell us now all about your connection with Mr. Hosmer Angel.'

As the great detective mopped his brow and climbed back into his armchair, very red-of-face and exhausted, I noticed a flush over Miss Sutherland's face. She picked nervously at the fringe of her jacket.

'I met him first at the gas-fitters' ball,' she said. 'They used to send Father tickets when he was alive, and then afterwards they remembered us, and sent them to Mother. Mr. Windibank did not wish to go. He never did wish us to go anywhere. He would get quite mad if I wanted so much as to join a Sunday school treat. But this time I was set on going, and I would go, for what right had he to prevent me? He said that folk were not fit for us to know, when all Father's friends were to be there. And he said that I had nothing fit to wear, when I had my purple plush that I had never so much as taken out of the drawer. At last, when nothing else would do, he went off to France upon the business of the firm, but we went, Mother and I, with Mr. Hardy, who used to be our Foreman, and it was there I met Mr. Hosmer Angel.'

'I suppose,' said Holmes, 'that when Mr. Windibank came back from France, he was very annoyed at your having gone to the ball.'

'Oh, well, surprisingly, he was very good about it. He laughed and shrugged his shoulders and said there was no use denying anything to a woman, for she would have her way.'

'I see. How very philosophical of him. Then, at the gas-fitters' ball you met, as I understand, this gentleman called Mr. Hosmer Angel.'

'Yes, sir. I met him that night, and he called next day to ask if we had got home all safe, and after that we met him – that is to say, Mr. Holmes, I met him twice for walks, but after that Father came back again, and Mr. Hosmer Angel could not come to the house anymore.'

'No? And why not?'

'Father wouldn't have any visitors if he could help it, and he used to say that a woman should be happy in her own family circle. But then, as I used to say to Mother, a woman wants her own circle to begin with, and I had not got mine yet.'

'But how about Mr. Angel? Did he make no attempt to see you?'

'Well, Father was off to France again in a week, and Hosmer wrote and said that it would be safer and better not to see each other until he had gone. We could write in the meantime, and he used to write every day. I intercepted the letters in the morning, so there was no need for father to know.'

'Were you engaged to the gentleman at this time?'

'We were engaged after the first walk that we took!' She giggled. '*Hosey* was a cashier in an office in Leadenhall Street!'

HOSEY?!

Holmes raised his eyebrows at me in reference to the affectionate nickname; this was enough to tell Holmes and I how far this relationship had progressed, the expression "going for the first walk" obviously a euphemism for "stuffing the turkey."

'What office?' Holmes enquired.

'That's the worst of it, Mr. Holmes, I don't know.'

'Never mind. Where did he live?'

'He slept on the premises.'

'Tsk! And you don't know the address?'

'No, except it was in Leadenhall Street.'

'Where did you address your letters, then?'

'To the Leadenhall Post Office, to be left until called for. He said that if they were sent to the office he would be chaffed by all the other clerks about having letters from a lady, so I offered to typewrite them, like he did his, but he wouldn't have that, for he said that when I wrote them they seemed to come from me but when they were typewritten he always felt that the machine had come between us. That will just show you how fond he was of me, Mr. Holmes, and the little things that he would think of.'

'It was most suggestive,' said Holmes. 'It has long been an axiom of mine that the little things are infinitely the most important. Can you remember any other little things about Mr. Hosmer Angel?'

'He was a very shy man, Mr. Holmes. He would rather walk with me in the evening than the daylight, for he said that he hated to be conspicuous. Very retiring and gentlemanly he was. Even his voice was gentle. He'd had the quinsy and swollen glands when he was young, he told me, and it had left him with a weak throat, and a hesitating, whispering fashion of speech. He was always well-dressed, very neat and plain, but his eyes were weak, just as mine are, and he wore tinted glasses against the glare.'

I couldn't help thinking that if *Hosey* had lived in the Stone Age, he wouldn't have lasted very long, he being a blind beetle with the quinsy – whatever that was – that could only whisper for help. He would have

The lamp post had more charisma than "Old Hosey!"

been dinosaur's supper in five minutes! But what was more disturbing, was that Miss Sutherland referred to him in the past tense. Maybe she knew that he was dead all along and wasn't telling us? Hmmm! Maybe this would be revealed later.

'What happened when Mr. Windibank, your Stepfather, retired to France?'

'Hosey came to the house again and proposed that we should marry before Father came back. He was in dreadful earnest, and made me swear, with both of my hands on his Testament...'

I think that was another euphemism...

'...that whatever happened I would always be true to him. Mother said that he was right to make me swear, and that it was a sign of passion. Mother was all in favour from the first and was even fonder of him than I was. Then, when they talked of marrying within the week, I began to ask about Father; but they both said never to mind about Father and just to tell him afterwards. Mother said she would make it all right with him. I didn't quite like that, Mr. Holmes. It seemed funny that I should ask his leave, as he was only a few years older than me; but I didn't want to do anything on the sly, so I wrote to Father at Bordeaux, where the Company has its French offices, but the letter came back to me on the very morning of the wedding.'

'It missed him then?'

'Yes, sir, for he had started to England just before it arrived.'

'Ha! That was unfortunate. Your wedding was arranged, then, for Friday. Was it to be in church?'

'Yes, sir, but very quietly. It was to be at St. Saviour's, near King's Cross, and we were to have breakfast afterwards at the St. Pancras Hotel. Hosmer came for us in a hansom, but as there were two of us, he put us both into it, and stepped himself into a four-wheeler which happened to be the only other cab in the street. We got in the church first, and when the four-wheeler drove up, we waited for him to step out, but no one was there! The cabman said he could not imagine what had become of him, for he had seen him get in with his own eyes. That was last Friday, Mr. Holmes, and I have never seen or heard anything since then to throw any light upon what became of him.'

'It seems to me that you have been very shamefully treated,' said Holmes.

'Oh, no, sir! He was too good and kind to leave me so. Why, all the morning he was saying to me that, whatever happened, I was to be true; and that even if something quite unforeseen occurred to separate us, I was always to remember that I was pledged to him, and that he would claim his pledge sooner or later. It seemed strange talk for a wedding morning, but what has happened since gives a meaning to it.'

'Most certainly it does. Your own opinion is, then, that some unforeseen catastrophe has occurred to him.'

'Yes, sir. I believe that he foresaw some danger, or else he would not have talked so. And then I think that what he foresaw happened.'

'But you have no notion as to what it could have been?'

'None.'

'One more question. How did your Mother take the matter?'

'She was angry and said that I was never to speak of the matter again.'

'And your Father? Did you tell him?'

'Yes, and he seemed to think, with me, that something had happened, and that I should hear of Hosmer again. As he said, what interest could anyone have in bringing me to the doors of the church, and then leaving me?'

What indeed?! I reckon he took another look at her, sized her up, and decided that he couldn't squeeze her through the front door.

'Now, if he had borrowed my money, or if he had married me and got my money settled on him, there might be some reason; but Hosey was very independent about money, and never would look at a shilling of mine. And yet what could have happened? And why would he not write? Oh, it drives me half mad to think of it! And I can't sleep a wink at night.'

She pulled a little handkerchief out of her muff – the one covering her hands, thank goodness – and began to sob heavily into it.

'I shall glance into this case for you,' said Holmes, rising, 'and I have no doubt that we shall reach some definite result.'

'Oh, really, Mr. Holmes? Why thank you! You are a true gent.' And she wiped her piping eye clear from any tears.

'Let the weight of the matter rest upon me now,' he continued. My weighty look of mock anguish caught Holmes's eye, but he proceeded unabated: 'And do not let your mind dwell upon it further. Above all, try to let Mr. Hosmer Angel vanish from your memory.'

'As he has done from your life.' I said, mournfully.

'Ohhhh!' she squealed and started to cry again. This was a bad situation. There was no predicting what she would do next. Holmes lifted his eyebrows to the heavens and gestured I should try to calm her down. I stood up and went to place my hands upon her bucking-and-diving shoulders as she sobbed her heart out. Luckily, after a while, my healing hands worked their magic and she became more placid. She looked up at Holmes.

'Do you think that I'll see him again, ever?' she quavered.

'No, I fear not,' said Holmes.

'AAWWWWW!' she bawled out, this time even more dramatically! Her gigantic frame heaved up and down, like there was an earthquake taking place beneath us.

'Steady on Holmes!' I cried, because I was in the danger zone.

'Steady as she goes there, Doctor!' he advised, most helpfully. And after an enormous amount of comforting, I managed to bring her back to her senses. I glared at Holmes, just to tell him that he should not put me through that type of trauma again.

'What has happened to him, Mr. Holmes?' she asked.

I glared some more!

'You must leave that question in my hands, Miss Sutherland. I should like an accurate description of him, and any letters of his which you can spare.'

'I advertised for him in Saturday's *Chronicle*,' said she. 'Here is the skip, and here are four letters from him.'

'Thank you. And your address?'

'31 Lyon Place, Camberwell.'

'Mr. Angel's address you never had; I understand. Where is your Father's place of business?'

'He travels for Westhouse & Marbank, the great claret importers of Fenchurch Street.'

'Now there's a man who landed the plum job!' said Holmes. 'Thank you for your statement. You have made it clearly. You will leave the papers here and remember the advice which I have given you. Let the whole incident be a sealed book, and do not allow it to affect your life.'

'You are very kind, Mr. Holmes, but I cannot do that. I shall be true to my Hosey. He shall find me all ready when he comes back!' And she laughed out loud.

I studied her, wobbling away, all jelly-like, and couldn't help thinking what an exciting homecoming prospect she was for Hosey. I thought about our new client some more, as she made merry of her own little joke, and I thought that maybe I was being too mean about her because for all the preposterousness and her vacuousness, there was something noble in the simple faith of our visitor which compelled our respect.

That was why I decided to pre-empt her potential embarrassment of trying to leave the apartment, because she was crammed into the Mummy Couch tighter than a sixpence in a Welshman's purse. As she prepared to launch, I darted forwards from my seat and dashed in behind her. I planted my foot upon the crossbar bridging the two rear legs of the chair and leaned heavily upon it. My plan worked perfectly, because when she went to stand up, she slipped out of the front of the chair with ease, like a salmon into a swim. Holmes noticed my noble gesture and nodded his appreciation because Miss Sutherland could not have been happier. She laid her papers down on the table, brushed herself down, smoothing her dress and adjusting her hat, before we walked towards the door to show her out. I whispered into Holmes's ear: 'That was a lot easier than I thought it would be,' I said, as we escorted our new client down the staircase towards the front door.

Holmes leaned close to me and murmured: 'The silk petticoat is a wonderful piece of lingerie, Watson.'

'And there was I thinking that we would need a cake!' I hissed back, but Holmes didn't laugh, and, although I had made this small riposte at the lowest volume, Miss Sutherland's ears twitched. She looked over her shoulder and lobbed me an embarrassing: 'I heard that Doctor Watson!' But, to her credit, she never broke step as she crossed the threshold and bade us goodbye.

We closed the door. Normally, we would have collapsed into laughter together but this time I was all on my own. For once, Holmes did not find it funny in the least way, so I tried to buck him up.

'I say, Holmes, just how *did* she hear me mention the cake?'

'Maybe God gave her acute hearing because she is a great, big fat woman?' and without further ado he walked back up the stairs. What had I said to upset him?

* * *

Later that morning we travelled by South Western railways to the contemporary town of Godalming. Holmes and I were lodged in the first-class compartment. We were making a pastoral journey through the Surrey countryside to visit his family, an event that I had been invited to accompany him upon. I had never met his parents or either of his siblings – Mycroft and Rachel – but that would be remedied today when I was the honoured guest at a landmark birthday celebration.

Holmes looked as if he was sitting for a portrait painter. He was quite a picture, dressed in Inverlochy tweed – the pale partridge grey, not the dark – with matching peaked cap – the dark partridge, not the pale. His cloak was a dogtooth manteau, piped with a tan doeskin trim, and he wore strong leather brogues with deep outsoles and pronounced welts, stoutly crafted for walking on rough terrain. He was all kitted-out for a day out in the Highlands. Sadly, we had only travelled as far as Woking.

I watched the great detective ingesting information from *The Times* whilst puffing on his large briar pipe. Clouds of blue smoke filled the compartment and funnelled out of the top window. I had attempted to converse with him, but he blocked me out with grunts and flashes of his eyes, flicking them away in a glance from the text to deliver me a "do not disturb" sign. However, when I asked him whose birthday we would be celebrating, he looked up from his newspaper and answered: 'My good Doctor, surely you have observed and deduced whose anniversary it is by now?' and then returned to his reading.

I sat opposite, in mute contemplation. I was a nervous man living in great trepidation: I was daunted by the prospect of a celebratory luncheon for an unknown person in the middle of a confluence of the extraordinary Holmes family, and to find myself sitting in the first-class compartment of the coach without a ticket. Therefore, not only was I struggling to guess the identity of the birthday boy or girl, I was also keeping a close eye on the corridor, in case we should hear the approach of a conductor and be confronted with a demand for payment. The journey, however, passed without interruption for money we did not have. We arrived at Godalming station just before noon to be greeted effusively by the Station Master, a young chap with a spring in his step and smart look in his eye. At first, I thought that he must have recognised us as the detectives from *The Strand* magazine, so I was not surprised by the warmth of his welcome, but then it became apparent that he didn't know us from Adam and he was collecting unpaid fares on behalf of the absentee conductor. Whilst I was mining my pockets for cash, Holmes gave me space to resolve the transaction and left me behind to find transport to our next destination. By the time I joined him on the concourse outside, he was sitting in the back of a dog cart, which was harnessed to a mangy-looking pony and an even mangier-looking driver. Holmes could see the disappointment creased all over my features, and he broke out the broadest of grins.

'Come, come dear Doctor, you are in the countryside now! The chance of finding a four-wheeler and a brace of Windsors this far from town is next to none. In these circumstances, this fine carriage is a Pullman of the highway and Burt, there, is our Casey Jones.'

Burt, the be-whiskered yokel, turned around to look at me and said: 'Your guvernor's bright. I told him that this fine dog cart is a Godsend! And do you know what he said?' "Yes, I can see that." And no more needed to be said. Can you see why it is a God-send?'

'For God's sakes' I said. 'NO! Because it hasn't got any shit in it?'

'There! Luxury!' said Holmes 'Hop in.'

They both laughed themselves to bits. I stepped up onto the plate. I thought to myself: what a curious and noticeable feature of the human mind it is that so often it will seize upon the most unimportant aspects in life, almost to the exclusion of anything else, just to cause amusement? This was, of course, all at my expense. My thoughts made my nose twitch and darkened my visage. This made them laugh even harder.

'Sit yourself down, just there,' pointed Holmes, 'and we shall enjoy a tour of the town and its reaches, as described by new best friend, Burt.'

With a sharp crack of the yokel's whip we set off. Burt followed the tow path next to the river Wey. We passed the church of St. Peter and St. Paul's on the right, trotted across a marsh by a mill, and headed in a northerly direction towards the village of Eashing. After half a mile or so we climbed a steep incline where many new houses were under construction. At the top it flattened out like a table and we soon swept into a driveway with a freshly planted avenue of trees. I deduced we were close to our destination.

'Watson, we have arrived at Charterhouse School. My Father is the Professor-in-Residence here,' said Holmes.

My mind was so distracted by this new landscape I blurted out: 'This is where your parents live?'

Holmes latched on like a salmon to a fly. He leaned forwards, lifted my bowler, tilted it on one side by my ear and shouted: 'THE CLUE IS IN THE JOB TITLE!'

I felt very stupid. Burt drove us through the school grounds, and I took a moment to ponder. This was the perfect distraction because the school was a remarkable sight, with its imposing buildings recently constructed in the neo-classical style. I wondered what it must be like to be educated in a seat of learning with such classical allusions, my own education having taken place at a modest establishment near Surbiton, and, at sixteen years my parents had packed me off to the army. After a while my mind turned back to the nagging question.

'Why is your Father a Professor-in-Residence, Holmes?'

'That, Watson, is an excellent question, ten times better than your last. Well done! He studies and practices nuclear physics.'

'I have never heard of it.'

'I am not surprised. Nuclear physics is a new discipline that studies the atom. It has scientists – top scientists – working day and night to define its very definition. In Germany, there is Herr Willhelm Röntgen. In France, Monsieur Becquerel, and here we have JJ Thomson in Oxford and in Canada the esteemed Dr. Ernest Rutherford. Here, in Godalming, you will soon be meeting Professor Julian Cornelius Bortzoy Holmes. He is the most advanced of all the nuclear physicists. Ha!' Holmes grinned excitedly and waved his finger at me. 'Daddy is the best!'

'Yes, of course… He would be, Holmes…' I said, whilst thinking: Goodness me! I was about to meet a man that I had never met before who was the leading light in a new doctrine about an atom, whatever that was, that I had never heard of. I was very confused! So, to unclutter my mind, I sat back and returned to admiring the beautiful architecture. The whole school may have been brand new, but it did not give that appearance. It was constructed with the most beautiful blend of sandstone, brick and clay that you could ever imagine. There were quadrants and cloisters all laid out cleverly in the Romanesque Revival style, with Doric columns, segmental arches, stone-mullioned windows, leaded lights and stained glass. Eventually, I ran out of architectural lexicon and my mind flitted back to the subject in hand.

'So, just how would you describe this new science called nuclear physics, Holmes?'

'It is far too complicated to explain to a medical layman such as yourself, Watson, in two minutes or so. Here we are! We have arrived at my parents' house. Daddy will tell you all about it instead.'

We pulled up outside a perfectly mundane house. It was a family home of about four or five bedrooms designed in a mock-Tudor style that was just one in a row of similar buildings, all spaced sparingly and evenly. Each one had a small garden at the front.

We jumped down from the dog cart. My friend marched straight towards the house. Once I had reminded Burt that we were returning to London that evening, and that he should be staying put whilst we enjoyed our luncheon, I followed Holmes up the pathway where a sharp rat-tat-tat had resulted in a butler opening the door. Already I was anxious about meeting these people but now I slowed down and simply observed the servant greeting my friend. He met Holmes with deferentiality, hands behind his back, but he was so short – probably only five and a quarter foot – it was hard to tell if he bowed or not. Just at that moment, I had a pre-conception of what the Holmes family would be like inside the house, a vision of tall, thin replicas of the great detective himself, all bossy, aloof and superior, with massive throbbing and pulsating foreheads. I was about to feel inadequate, both in height and intellect.

Holmes stepped inside just as I arrived on the doorstep. I took a look at the butler. He was a little runt of a man, fully regaled in coat and pinstripe, old and bald, with ginger tufts of hair sticking out of the side of his head. The bulbous nose, thin lips and teapot ears placed him firmly in the servant class. He adjusted his spectacles, beamed up at me and thrust out his hand. What a cheek! I ignored it.

'Welcome to Buck-ing-ham Palace!' he announced, in a broad Welsh brogue. I surveyed the diminutive edifice in one glance and shot him as much of a smile as I thought that his pathetic joke deserved.

'Hardly!' I said. 'I am surprised the family have enough space to fit you servants into it!'

He chuckled amiably. 'Rrr-ight you are there, sir!' he said, and then added: 'I rrr-espect a man with a rrr-ibald sense of humour!'

'My name is Watson. Doctor John Watson.'

'Yes, I know that Doctor. Tidy! Very tidy!' he declared, all Celtic and affable-like. 'Just as Master Sherlock rrr-elat-ed to me, sir.' I took a different look at him. He had laughed at just the right level to make me feel comfortable but without drawing attention to himself. And this man had a humble respect for doctors. Hmmm! This servant was a consummate professional. I gave him a nod, one professional to another. He nodded back. We knew our station in this life, without the use of words.

I entered the narrow hallway. Here, I found just what I had predicted: Sherlock Holmes in conversations with his siblings. There was a handsome man of similar build and age to himself but with an even larger forehead, and a woman who must have been six feet two in her bare feet with wild, raven-black hair. Holmes caught sight of my arrival and broke into their quorum.

'Mycroft, let me introduce you to my good friend, John Watson.'

They turned around to greet me. The woman had a strikingly beautiful face that captured me instantly – I couldn't take my eyes off her – but then the dashing Mycroft stepped forwards and shook my hand with a very firm grip.

'His *only* friend!' he quipped. He laughed, infectiously, and we all laughed with him. My goodness, this man exuded a supreme confidence! This was an incarnation of Sherlock Holmes but with a powerful dose of bonhomie added to the mix.

'John, this is Rachel.' Holmes held out his hand and presented his sister. I was fortunate to look at her because she was a beautiful sight. Rachel wore a deep red, silk, brocade dress that displayed her long abdomen perfectly, and in a thoroughly thought-provoking way! She wore long, green, velvet gloves that covered her forearms and finished on her biceps. She moved closer to me and held out a velvety hand. I lifted it gently into mine and looked into her face. As I brought it up to my lips, I heard a distinctive 'Mmmm!' And for the second time that day I felt a bolt of electricity shoot through my body as my heart leapt into her lagoon-like eyes.

'How simply delightful to meet you, John,' she breathed huskily. 'I heard that you were coming but Sherlock has told us so much of *absolutely nothing* about you.' She licked her lips, I swear! 'So please, you must tell me *absolutely everything* about yourself.'

'That will be my pleasure,' I stuttered out.

'Well, it will not be ours, Doctor!' joked Holmes, as he warmed up his siblings to join in with his ritual teasing. 'John was in the army. Therefore, you will have heard it all a thousand times before. The tour of Afghanistan. The warring hill tribes. The Gilzais. The Ghazis. The Jezail bullet in the leg.'

'That's the army for you!' quipped Mycroft, but Rachel threw the laughing brothers a javelin from each of her emerald-green eyes.

'Sherlock! Mycroft! Don't you mock our guest so, my cynical brothers! John did not invite a Jezail bandit to shoot a bullet into his leg.' She stepped in closer and grabbed me by the arm, pulling me in to her face. 'But, dear John, I am sure that you suffered bravely as the burning lead buried itself into your leg... somewhere down there! I shall hang on to your every word, I promise.'

Suddenly, I was barged roughly aside. The Celtic butler squeezed in between Rachel and I, separating our brief intimacy in an instant. He was wringing his hands excitedly.

'The Brrrrrr-ec-on lamb has been be rrr-oaaa-sted to purrr-fection!' he announced, with such effusive delivery that the MC at The Lyceum could have gone into retirement. 'I shall go and rrr-eee-scue its succulent flesh from the fiery rrrr-oasting dish! Now just so you rrr-eaaa-dy yourselves fooo-rrr some rrr-oasted potatoes. And brrr-aiiii-sed brrr-o-cc-oli! Don't loiter here, boyos! Go and find your Mother and introduce our honoured guest.'

And with the shock revelation that the little Welsh butler was, in fact, Professor Julian Holmes, I allowed Rachel to push her arm through mine and lead me towards the sitting room.

* * *

We walked into the sitting room. There, sprawled out on a two-seater couch – or maybe it was a three-seater, I just couldn't tell – was Mrs. Wendy Holmes. She was over six feet tall and about twenty-five stones. She was a very large woman indeed, dwarfing even our client, Miss Sutherland... Oh my goodness! I stopped dead in my tracks. I just stared at his Mother, the blood draining from my face, a cold sweat breaking out on my brow. My mind raced back to the morning – I had made one big, bad, joke after another about fat people. I looked over my shoulder and Holmes, sure enough, was wearing his 'mortally offended but tolerant' face, and when he caught my eye, he sighed over-dramatically and then smiled evilly at my inner torment.

We had stopped in front of Mother, but just as Rachel was about to introduce me, Holmes dashed in front and kissed his Mother on her cheek.

'Good morning, Mother. You look well. May I introduce Watson? He makes jokes about fat people.'

'Don't be ridiculous, Sherlock!' said Rachel. 'Mummy, this is his friend, John, and he doesn't make jokes about...people.'

'Please excuse me if I don't get up,' said Mrs. Holmes as she leaned forwards to take my hand. 'It is my sciatica. It causes me no end of trouble.'

Had I mentioned sciatica being the side-effect of grossly overweight people this morning? The grin on Sherlock Holmes's face answered that question! I shook her pudgy hand. 'Mrs. Holmes, it is my pleasure. May I suggest some exercises for your condition that will stretch your piriformis?'

Mrs. Holmes raised her eyebrows in inquisitive surprise. I thought I should clarify my suggestions.

'The piriformis being some small, supportive muscles positioned around the spine. If you were to lay on the floor, pull your legs up to your chest and roll from side to side I am sure you will relieve the pain.'

Mrs. Holmes raised her eyebrows even higher and then scowled. 'I am not sure whether to ask you to leave!'

'Mummy,' said Rachel, coming to my rescue whilst Holmes just smirked. 'John is a Doctor of Medicine.'

'Is this true?' she asked, looking into my eyes.

'Indeed, it is.'

Her face lit up and she smiled. 'My apologies, Doctor Watson! You must find me rude and presumptuous.' She threw her arms up with excitement. 'I shall do exactly as you suggest!'

'Mummy is a Doctor of Botany,' whispered Rachel, but loud enough for everybody to hear her.

'Everybody here is a doctor!' interjected Mycroft, raising his arms up towards the ceiling, just like Mother. 'I am a Doctor of Anthropology. Rachel, a Doctor of Philosophy. Sherlock, a Doctor of Chemistry.'

'And I am a doctor of Sunday lunch!' said the Professor. 'And it is all rrr-eady for you!'

We turned to look at Professor Holmes standing at the kitchen door, now wearing his striped apron and chef's hat and holding up a roasting fork in triumph.

I noticed the great detective slip out past him, but my thoughts were interrupted by Rachel's sparkling enthusiasm.

'Daddy is being modest. He is a *cordon bleu*.'

'My word!' I exclaimed. 'We are in for a treat.'

'And it is another reason why I am so fat,' confessed Wendy Holmes, 'and my sciatica nerve is so crimped.'

Sherlock reappeared at his Mother's side. He shot me a mischievous glance and then crouched down again to talk to her. 'That is not quite correct, is it Mother? Father's cooking is undeniably excellent but that is not the reason for your life-threatening condition. Believe me, the good Dr. Watson here will try to be sympathetic to your *true* affliction, just as he was this morning with one of my clients.' He turned to face me. 'Your diagnosis of this morning was "she is a big, fat woman," wasn't it Doctor?'

I ignored him and stooped down to consult Mrs. Holmes confidentially. 'What is your diagnosis?'

'I have been told that it is Cushing's Syndrome,' declared Wendy Holmes solemnly.

My heart fell out onto the floor. 'The over-active adrenal gland condition? I am so sorry...'

'There is nothing for you to apologise about, Watson. My Mother has been forced to suffer obesity abuse for many years!'

'Oh no, Holmes! I meant nothing by it...'

'Is that so? Here, maybe you could tempt her through to the dining room with this...'

I was feeling low, very low indeed. Ever since I had set foot in the Holmes's family home, I had put that foot in it! The butler was Father; the Colossus of Godalming was Mother; I had a most fervent attraction to my friend's Sister that was bound to cause stress in the future. I was downtrodden, but nothing could prepare me for what happened next.

You remember that Holmes had disappeared to the kitchen? Well, the devil himself now thrust his hand towards me and dropped a giant slice of chocolate cake into my hand! I did not know what to do, which way to turn. I just goggled at it! Then, I heard the guffaws of laughter. I looked up. They were gathered around me, the entire Holmes family, all enjoying this joke together, the joke at my expense. Even Wendy Holmes was creased up, piping tears. Sherlock Holmes had been taking me for a complete and utter goose!

'I see, I see, I see...,' I said, as the wave of realisation ebbed over me and I relaxed from my crouch to sit upon the parquet floor. I was much calmer now. I smiled up at them one by one, all laughing and smiling at the success of their set-up and the easy access of my gullibility.

'I see it all now,' I said, and I did, clear as Waterford crystal. 'I understand. This is a type of initiation ceremony. Ha! Very good...'

And with that resolution in mind I came up with an idea that might show me up to be a good sport. I jumped up with a spring in my step, like a newborn lamb, and I addressed them all.

'Don't forget, for twelve years I had a career in the army!' I announced.

Carefully, and slowly, I presented the cake to Wendy Holmes, cheekily, my arm outstretched to her holding the chocolate temptation, whilst I gradually crabbed my way backwards, towards the dining room door.

'Come along Mrs. Holmes! May I call you Wendy? Just look at this delicious cake, Wendy. Moist! Choc-o-late. Sponge. Come on, now… You know you want some! Here! Come along now…!'

'He's one of us!' cried Professor Holmes. All of a sudden, the room erupted with laughter. Every member of the family wanted to shake my hand. Even the Colossus of Godalming shook off her sciatica and patted my arm. And Rachel gave me a hug that caused a nasty trouser moment.

And that is how I became the fourth sibling of the notorious Holmes family.

* * *

The Professor was a very competent cook. He produced five courses of delicious food. After three courses I felt a different person. The pre-visit anxiety about meeting the family and the pre-luncheon desolation concerns about my fat-person jokes were long forgotten. My position at the table between Rachel and Wendy was warm and friendly. I relaxed into the comfortable, family ambience. It was Rachel who created the first topic of conversation and it was about names. She chided Holmes, and then me, about how we addressed one another, each one of us resorting to surnames or, in my instance, my profession as a doctor and, in Holmes's case, his occupation as a detective.

My sense of humour made me very popular amongst fat people.

'Sherlock. Surely you do not still address John as Watson?'

'He is Watson.'

'I am not playing one of those silly word games of yours, Sherlock. JOHN is not a stranger. JOHN is no longer in the army. He is not your inferior. You must call him by his first name.'

Holmes was taken aback. To witness the great detective on the ropes was a rare moment indeed. I grinned at him across the table in silent facetiousness, until I was caught by Rachel.

'And you, John Watson, can wipe that smile from your face! Don't inflate my brother's ego by calling him "the great detective" or the like. He may be a competent analyst of data, in his own field of expertise, but it makes him even more intolerable! Please, just address him as Sherlock.'

'But is it not too familiar?'

'Too familiar? You live together in the same apartment. You live like husband and wife.'

'I have never met another Sherlock. One could announce: "Sherlock!" across a crowded room and nobody else will look up.'

'It is queer thing indeed...' remarked the Professor, as we hung on for his very next word, 'to not refer to one another by your Christian names.'

From this moment on, we resolved to fulfil the Professor's wishes. But I had one question from that morning that I was curious to know the answer, and that was where, on Earth, they had found that name Sherlock.

'When he was born, we quite liked having him in the home,' said Wendy. 'But he had a strange look about him. He was very hairy.'

'Like a chimpanzee?'

'Keep quiet, Watson.'

'We were undecided upon a name. It was his Nanny who made the decision for us.'

Suddenly, Sherlock became decidedly agitated. He up his hands. 'No, Mother, that is enough. This family saga is not for a stranger's "entertainment."'

Mycroft and Rachel booed in opposition, encouraging the Professor to jump up from his chair. He clapped his hands and rubbed then together with glee, relishing the opportunity laid out before him.

'Oh, yes, it is. Your friend, the doctor, would love to hear about this!' exclaimed the Professor. 'This is what family gatherings are for — first-class humiliation! Now, let me tell you all about it...'

Sherlock sat back in his chair, deflated. He dropped his head onto his chest and closed his eyes in silent resignation.

'It was his loooong black hair that caught his Nanny's eye,' rolled the Professor. 'One day, Wendy and I went to visit our little chimpanzee in his nursery. We found his Nanny combing his loooong, locks of hair with one hand. In the other, she held a pair of loooong, sh-aarrr-p sci-sso-rrrs! Then, to our surprise, she liff-ted the in-fant by his hair. In one, swift, movement, she CHOPPED it all off! She held it up above her head in tri-umph! She shoo-ook it! She ululated, like...' The Professor cocked his head back, opened his mouth, and let fly. 'OW-WOW-WOW-WOW-WOOOH!' His audience laughed and applauded politely, all except for Sherlock, and then he leaned forwards to finish off his saga. 'Then, she threw it into her cauldron, and announced to us that his name would be "sh-eeee-rr lock."'

Whether the story was true of not, is irrelevant. It was a highly entertaining way to spend luncheon!

'Goodness!' I said. 'Were you not concerned about the sanity of this woman?'

'Ha! Ah nooo... She was a witch, of that there is no doubt, but a harmless one, and she was a very fine wet-nurse.'

'And Mycroft?' I asked?

'I was born in a Scottish cottage!' Said Mycroft jauntly. Everybody laughed. I made the most of it and nodded my head to Mycroft, acknowledging his wit.

'I don't think so, Mycroft!' I exclaimed, only to be stopped in my tracks by the great detective.

'No... John... he *was* born in a Scottish cottage.'

The laughter lifted in volume and filled the room. Oh, what a jolly time we were having!

'So, therefore, along the same lines...' I said, 'Rachel must have been born in a synagogue?'

The laughter died away, petering out rapidly to silence, an angel passing through a room in Godalming on his way to Coventry.

'I'll fetch the pudding,' said the Professor.

During the hazelnut meringue with apricot dressing, we moved on to more powerful topics. It was a joy to behold the five gigantic intellects in one space, sometimes harnessed together, but often competing against one another in a contest of supreme one-upmanship. But, also, it was extremely awkward for me because I was treated as an equal and they sought my opinions. I didn't have a clue what they were talking about! Typically, the process was thus: each topic was debated and resolved in essence, and then each member of the family took it in turn to ask me for approval before a final conclusion. It was started by the question of measuring the Earth's mass and the accuracy of Schiehallion against Cavendish, culminating in Mycroft asking me: "Would you not agree, Doctor, that Henry's experiment made a mockery of the Scottish mountain?" I didn't know. Then, Wendy Holmes quizzed me thus: "Unless dear John has a different opinion upon whether the Schmeissneria plant was the earliest angiosperm?" To which, annoyingly, Sherlock pronounced the genus to be "a Ginkgoaceae" and Wendy agreed that it was. I had no answer to that. Later, the Professor asked me to come down on his side in the argument with his family about how to split the atom. There was that word "atom" again, and I didn't know what he was talking about. The only respite was an intimate conversation I had with Rachel at my side and, secretly, I suspected she was having a femininity crisis and was seeking masculine company. To my delight she seemed to have selected me as her medicine.

'After lunch, John, we shall go out for walk in the countryside' she said. Then, she leaned in close and whispered to me: 'I must lose some of this enormous lunch, and I don't intend to shed it all by walking. I know a place that we can go to.' This was a message that I understood loud and clear, and I became very excited – Rachel had caused a throbbing of my trouser bone!

Unfortunately, Sherlock had overheard our discourse, and he became determined to thwart the type of intercourse we had in mind. At the end of the meal, Rachel stood up and announced our intention to take a turn through the rural walks of the school grounds. The dutiful chaperone sprang from his seat saying what a capital idea it was, and he would be joining us. This, in turn, caused the Professor to propose a guided tour of the grounds and a visit to his laboratory. Mycroft offered to push Wendy's bath-chair and that was the end of our plans of afternoon intimacy. I gave Rachel my most resigned look and she returned the same to me, but using those gorgeous, green lagoon eyes. With my hopes dashed, my heart sunk, and my trouser bone restored to barracks, we embarked upon a healthy, Sunday afternoon ambulation around Charterhouse School.

* * *

The next morning, we were back in Baker Street, in conference over the Sutherland case. It was just after breakfast. Sherlock Holmes sat silent for a few minutes, with his fingertips still pressed together, his legs stretched out in front of him, and his gaze directed upwards to the ceiling. Then he took down from the rack the old and oily clay pipe, which was to him as a counsellor, and having lit it he leaned

Professor Julian Cornelius Bortzoy Holmes was such a brilliant physicist I didn't understand a word he said!

back in his chair, with the thick blue cloud wreaths spinning up from him, and a look of infinite languor in his face.

'Quite an interesting study, that maiden,' he observed.

'Rachel is a maiden?'

'Not my Sister, you dog, Watson! Miss Sutherland.'

'I am not sure she is a maiden, Sherlock.'

'I think you will find that she is. And stop calling me Sherlock.'

'Sorry, Holmes. I was only thinking of yesterday's conversation and resolution.'

'This is not yesterday, Doctor; it is today. With regards to Miss Sutherland, I suspect the innuendo of intimacy she included in her account about her relationship with Mr. Angel was steeped in dreams rather than devilment. But it might be relevant because I found her more interesting than her little problem, which, by the way, is rather a trite one. You will find parallel cases, if you consult my index, in Andover in '77, and there was something of the sort in The Hague last year. Old as is the idea, however, there were one or two details which were new to me. But the maiden herself was most instructive.'

'You appeared to read a good deal upon her which was quite invisible to me,' I remarked.

'Not invisible, but unnoticed, Watson. You did not know where to look, and so you missed all that was important. I can never bring you to realise the importance of sleeves, the suggestiveness of thumbnails, or the great issues that may hang from a bootlace. Now what did you gather from that woman's appearance? Describe it.'

Once again, we had arrived at the moment in a mystery when I would be embarrassed by my inferior deductive powers via a humiliation ritual instigated by the great detective. But I had learned to look at these situations from my perspective. He thought that he was teaching me a lesson from a position of superior intellect, whereas I regarded myself as his sounding-board, and it was his *only way* to distil his own observations and package them into a deduction. I had become an essential element of his detective work. In other words, I reckoned he needed me more than I needed him!

'Well, she had a slate-coloured, broad-brimmed straw hat,' I said, 'with a feather of a brickish red. Her jacket was black, with black beads sewn upon it, and a fringe of little black ornaments. Her dress was brown, rather darker than coffee colour, with a little purple plush at the neck and sleeves. Her gloves were greyish and were worn through at the right forefinger. Her boots I didn't observe. She had small, round, hanging gold ear-rings, and a general air of being fairly well to do, in a vulgar, comfortable, easy-going way.'

Sherlock Holmes clapped his hands softly together and chuckled.

'So relays the cub fashion reporter of the Baker Street Times!' quipped Holmes. 'You are coming along wonderfully. You have really done very well indeed. Sadly, you have missed everything of importance, but you have hit upon the method, and you have a quick eye for colour. Never trust to general impressions, my boy, but concentrate yourself upon details. My first glance is always a woman's sleeve; in a man it is perhaps better first to take the knee of the trouser. As you observe, this woman had plush upon her sleeves, which is a most useful material for showing traces. The double line a little above the wrist, where the typewriter presses against the table, was beautifully defined. The sewing machine, of the hand type, leaves a similar mark, but only on the left arm, and on the side of it farthest from the thumb, instead of being right across the broadest part, as this was. I then glanced at her face and observing the dint of a pince-nez at either side of her nose, I ventured a remark upon short sight and typewriting, which seemed to surprise her.'

'She was more surprised by your comment about her gigantic boobs. It was nothing to do with her myopia.'

'It still surprised me.'

'It still surprised her!'

'But surely it was very obvious. I was then much surprised... *and* interested on glancing down to observe that, though the boobs which she was wearing...'

'You mean "boots" she was wearing?'

'Oh? Yes...the boots she was wearing... were unlike each other, they were really odd ones, the one having a slightly decorated toecap, and the other a plain one.'

'When it comes to fashionable footwear, you are quite the Manalo Sputnik, Holmes!'

'Don't be silly, Watson, how could she possibly afford a pair of Sputniks on one hundred a year?

Anyway, one was buttoned only in the two lower buttons out of five, and the other at the first, third and fifth. Now, when you see boots like this, what is the great deduction? Doctor?'

'That one breast is larger than the other.'

Holmes sighed. Deeply. 'How can you be certain?'

'Because I am a doctor.'

'But that is not the great deduction I am seeking. Think, Doctor! When you see that a young lady, otherwise neatly dressed, has come away from home with odd boots, half-buttoned, the great deduction that I was looking for you to say was that she came away in a hurry.'

'Yes, that too. And what else?' I asked, keenly interested, as I always was, by my friend's incisive reasoning, although I still thought that my different sized boobs deduction to be totally relevant.

'I noted, in passing, that she had written a note before leaving home, but after being fully dressed. You observed that her right glove was torn at the forefinger, but you did not apparently see that both glove and finger were stained with violet ink. She had written in a hurry and dipped her pen too deep. It must have been this morning, or the mark would not remain clear upon the finger. All this is amusing, though rather elementary, but I must go back to business, Watson. Would you mind reading me the advertised description of Mr. Hosmer Angel.'

'Old Hosey? Why, surely it will be a big nose and curly hair?'

'There are no pre-conceptions here. We work from facts. Read it, Doctor'

'Of course, Holmes.'

I held a little printed slip to the light. "Missing," it said, "on the morning of the 14th, a gentleman named Hosmer Angel. About 5ft 7in. in height; strongly built, sallow complexion." 'I'll bet he wishes he'd eaten more greens, eh?'

'Get on with it!'

'"Black hair. A little bald in the centre, bushy black side whiskers and moustache; tinted glasses." Tsk! Really? "Slight infirmity of speech. Was dressed, when last seen, in black frockcoat faced with silk, black waistcoat, gold Albert chain, and grey Harris tweed trousers, with brown gaiters over elastic-sided boots. Known to have been employed in an office in Leadenhall Street. Anybody bringing…" etc. etc.'

'That will do,' said Holmes.

'That's all you are getting,' I replied, as I dropped the slip back onto the table.

'Now, to the letters…' He continued glancing over them. 'They are very commonplace. Absolutely no clue in them to Mr. Angel, save that he quotes Balzac once more. There is one remarkable point, however, which will no doubt strike you.'

'They are typewritten,' I remarked.

'Not only that, but the signature is typewritten. Look at the neat little "Hosmer Angel" at the bottom. There is a date you see, but no superscription, except Leadenhall Street, which is rather vague. The point about the signature is very suggestive – I fact, we may call it conclusive.'

'Of what?'

'My dear fellow, it is possible you do not see how strongly it bears upon the case?'

'I cannot say that I do, unless it were that he wished to be able to deny his signature if an action for breach of promise were instituted.'

'No, that was not the point. However, I shall write two letters which should settle the matter. One to a firm in the City, the other is to the young lady's Stepfather, Mr. Windibank, asking him whether he could meet us here at six o'clock tomorrow evening. It is just as well that we should do business with the male relatives. And now, Doctor, we can do nothing until the answers to those letters come, so we may put our little problem upon the shelf for the interim and put our feet up.' He re-ignited his clay pipe and pup-pup-pupped himself into a bonfire.

'But hold on,' says I, 'wouldn't it be a good idea to write the letters so that we may receive the answers?'

'Keenly observed, Watson! We shall make a detective of you yet.'

Holmes placed the pipe on the monkey's paw and rose up from his seat. He carried it over to the bureau without, seemingly, a care in the world. He picked up a pen and then sat back in the captain's chair and puffed on the pipe again. Clearly, he was in deep pontification about what to write. I studied his languid profile. I had so many reasons to believe in my friend's subtle powers of reasoning, and extraordinary energy in action, that I felt that he must have some solid grounds for the assured and easy demeanour with which he treated this singular mystery which he had been called upon to fathom. Only once had I known him to fail, in the case of the King of Bohemia and of the Irene Adler photograph, hence my account of that mystery being *A Balls-Up in Bohemia*, but when I looked back to the weird business of the *Sign of Four*, and the extraordinary circumstances connected with the *Study in Scarlet*, I felt that it would be a strange tangle indeed which he could not unravel. He took no notice of me when I departed to attend my surgery in South Kensington. I left him pup-pup-pupping on his black clay pipe with the conviction that when I came again that evening, I would find that he held in his hands all the clues which would lead up to the identity of the disappearing bridegroom of Miss Mary Sutherland.

A medical crisis of great gravity was engaging my professional attention at the time; and the whole of the day I was busy at the bedside of the sufferer. It was not until close upon six o'clock that I found myself free and was able to spring into a hansom and drive to Baker Street, half afraid that I might be too late to assist at the *dénouement* of the little mystery. I found Sherlock Holmes alone, however, half asleep, with his long, thin, form curled up in the recesses of his armchair. A formidable array of bottles and test-tubes, with the pungent cleanly smell of hydrochloric acid, told me that he had spent his day in the chemical work which was so dear to him.

'Well, have you solved it?' I asked, as I entered.

'Yes. It was the bisulphate of baryta.'

'No, no, the mystery!' I cried.

'Oh, that? I thought of the salt that I have been working upon. There was never any mystery in the matter, though, as I said yesterday, some of the details are of interest. The only drawback is that there is no law, I fear, that can touch the scoundrel.'

'Who was he, then, and what was his object in deserting Miss Sutherland?'

The question was hardly out of my mouth and Sherlock had not yet opened his lips to reply, when we heard a heavy footfall in the passage, and a tap at the door.

'That, Watson, does not sound like the dainty instep of Miss Sutherland!'

'Well, her instep wouldn't be too dainty, would it Holmes, carrying all that condition?'

He looked at me with raised eyebrows.

'Sorry...'

'That is the girl's Stepfather, if I am not mistaken,' he continued. 'He has written to me to say that he would be here before six. Here is Mr. James Windibank.'

'Ah! Mr. Windy-Pants, at last!'

'Ha! Quite so, Watson! But be quiet now... Come in!'

The man who entered was a sturdy middle-sized fellow, some thirty years of age, clean shaven, and sallow skinned, with a bland, insinuating manner, and a pair of wonderfully sharp and penetrating grey eyes. He shot a questioning glance at each of us, placed his shiny top-hat upon the sideboard, and, with a slight bow, sidled down into the nearest chair.

'Good evening, Mr. James Windibank,' said Holmes. 'I think that this typewritten letter is from you, in which you made an appointment with me for six o'clock!'

'Yes, sir, I am afraid that I am a little late, but I am not quite my own master, you know. I am sorry that Miss Sutherland has troubled you about this little matter, for I think it is far better not to wash linen of this sort in public. It was quite against my wishes that she came, but she is a very excitable, impulsive girl, as you may have noticed, and she is not easily controlled when she has made up her mind on a point. Of course, I do not mind you so much, as you are not connected with the official police, but it is not pleasant to have a family misfortune like this noised abroad. Besides, it is a useless expense, for how could you possibly find this Hosmer Angel?'

'On the contrary said Holmes quietly; 'I have every reason to believe that I will succeed in the discovering of Mr. Hosmer Angel.'

Mr. Windibank gave a violent start and dropped his gloves. 'I am delighted to hear it,' he said.

'It is a curious thing,' remarked Holmes, 'that a typewriter has really quite as much individuality as a man's handwriting. Unless they are quite new, not two of them write exactly alike. Some letters get more worn than others, and some wear only on one side. Now, you remark in this note of yours, Mr. Windibank, that in every case there is some little slurring over of the "e" and a slight defect in the tail of the "r." There are fourteen other characteristics, but those are the more obvious.'

'We do all our correspondence with this machine at the office, and no doubt it is a little worn,' our visitor answered, glancing keenly at Holmes with his bright little eyes.

'And now I will show you what is really a very interesting study, Mr. Windibank,' Holmes continued. 'I think of writing another little monograph some of these days on the typewriter and its relation to crime. It is a subject to which I have devoted some little attention. I have here four letters which purport to come from the missing man. They are all typewritten. In each case, not only are the "e's" slurred and the "r's" tailless, but you will observe, if you care to use my magnifying lens, that the fourteen other characters to which I have alluded are there as well.'

Mr. Windibank sprang out of his chair and picked up his hat. 'I cannot waste time over this sort of fantastic talk, Mr. Holmes,' he said. 'If you can catch the man, catch him and let me know when you have done it.'

'Certainly,' said Holmes, stepping over and turning the key in the door. 'I let you know, then, that I have caught him!'

'What! Where?' shouted Mr. Windibank, turning white to his lips, and glancing about him like a rat in a trap.

'Oh, it won't do – really, it won't,' said Holmes suavely. 'There is no possible getting out of it, Mr. Windibank. It is quite too transparent, and it was a very bad compliment when you said it was impossible for me to solve so simple a question. That's right! Sit down! And let us talk it over.'

Our visitor collapsed into a chair with a ghastly face and a glitter of moisture on his brow. 'It – it's not actionable,' he stammered.

'I am very much afraid that it is not. But between ourselves, "Mister Windy-Pants" – as Dr. Watson calls you here. It was as cruel, and selfish, and heartless a trick in a petty way as ever came before me.'

'I say, you two, I never did!'

Our visitor turned and glared at me. 'WINDY-PANTS?! How dare you! I haven't been called that since I was at school!'

'The Doctor is quite juvenile in his outlook, I can assure you,' said Holmes, flashing his eyes defiantly at me.

'It was YOU who coined the phrase, Mr. Holmes!' said Windy-Pants, jabbing his forefinger at the great detective. I suppressed a smirk at his distress.

'Yes, and in this instance, it is a nickname far too kind and generous!' said Holmes, jabbing an even longer finger in return. 'Now… Enough of this name-calling! Let me just run over the course of events, and you will contradict me if I go wrong.'

Windy-Pants sat huddled up in his chair, with his head sunk upon his breast, like one who is utterly crushed. Holmes sat in a chair by the fire and stuck his feet up on the corner of the mantelpiece, which was a long way up, but he had very long legs. Then, leaning back with his hands in his pockets, he began talking, rather to himself, as it seemed, rather than to us.

'The man married a woman very much older than himself for her money,' said he, 'and he enjoyed the use of the money of the daughter as long as she lived with them. It was a considerable sum for people in their position, and the loss of it would have made a serious difference. It was worth an effort to preserve it. The daughter was of a good, amiable disposition, but affectionate and warm-hearted in her ways, so that it was evident that with her fair personable advantages, and her little income, she would not be allowed to remain single long. Now her marriage would mean, of course, the loss of a hundred a year, so what does her stepfather do to prevent it? He takes the obvious course of keeping her at home and forbidding her to seek the company of people of her own age. But soon he found that that would not answer for ever. She became restive, insisted upon her rights, and finally announced her positive intention of going to a certain ball. What does her clever stepfather do then? He conceives an idea more creditable to his head than his heart. With the connivance and assistance of his wife he disguised himself, covered those keen eyes with tinted glasses, masked the face with a moustache and a pair of bushy whiskers, sunk that clear voice into an insinuating whisper, and, doubly secure on account of the girl's short sight, he appears as Mr. Hosmer Angel, and keeps off the other lovers by making love himself.'

'Making love to your Step-daughter?!' I cried. 'YOU BOUNDER, SIR!'

'It was only a joke at first,' groaned our visitor. 'We never thought that she would have been so carried away.'

'Very likely not,' said Holmes, and he picked up his narrative in the third person. 'However, that may be, the young lady was very decidedly carried away, and having quite made up her mind that her stepfather was in France, the suspicion of treachery never for an instant entered her mind. She was flattered by the gentleman's attentions, and the effect was increased by the loudly expressed admiration of her mother. Then Mr. Hosmer Angel began to call, for it was obvious that the matter should be pushed as far as it would go, if a real effect were to be produced. There were meetings, and an engagement, which would finally secure the girl's affections from turning towards anyone else. But the deception could not be kept up for ever. These pretended journeys to France were rather cumbrous. The thing to do was clearly to bring the business to an end in such a dramatic manner that it would leave a permanent impression upon the young lady's mind and prevent her from looking upon any other suitor for some time to come. Hence those vows of fidelity exacted upon a Testament, and hence also the wedding. James Windibank wished Miss Sutherland to be so bound to Hosmer Angel, and so uncertain as to his fate, that for ten years to come, at any rate, she would not listen to another man. As far as the church door he brought her, and then, as he could go no further, he conveniently vanished away by the old trick of stepping in at one door of a four-wheeler, and out at the other.'

Holmes lent over and stared straight at the culprit. 'I think that that was the chain of events, Mr. Windy-Pants!'

Unbeknown to me, an angry Miss Sutherland spied on us from my bedroom. She heard the confession of Windy-Pants.

'DON'T CALL ME THAT!' shouted our visitor, who had recovered something of his assurance while Holmes had been talking. He rose from his chair now with a cold sneer upon his pale face. 'Or I shall get very angry!' said he. 'What you say may be so, or it may not, Mr. Holmes, but if you are so very sharp you ought to be sharp enough to know that it is you who are breaking the law now, and not me. I have done nothing actionable from the first, but as long as you keep that door locked you lay yourself open to an action for assault and illegal constraint.'

'The law cannot, as you say, touch you,' said Holmes, unlocking and throwing open the door, 'yet there never was a man who deserved punishment more. If the young lady has a brother or a friend, he ought to lay a whip across your shoulders'. 'By Jove!' he continued, flushing up at the sight of the bitter sneer upon the man's face, 'it is not part of my duties to my client, but here's a riding crop handy, and I think I shall just treat myself to—' He took two swift steps towards the whip, and just as he grasped it there was a clomp! clomp! clomp! in the passage outside, which turned out to be the not-so-dainty instep of Miss Sutherland. Suddenly, there she was, filling the door space with her colossal frame, her face all twisted, puce and angry!

'GIVE ME THAT, Mr. Holmes!' she bellowed. 'So, I may deal with Mr. Windibank in my own way.'

'Here it is,' said Holmes, and tossed the crop in the air past the villain's face, whose expression had now changed to one of extreme distress, to land in Miss Sutherland's hand. 'And, by the way, we call him "Windy-Pants."'

For the first time that day, Windy-Pants didn't rise to the nickname gibe; he was far too distracted by reconnaissance of his unfortunate situation, and where best to find his escape route. He was trapped between Holmes and Miss Sutherland, with me standing further back in the room. His eyes flashed side-to-side, and then his head turned left and right. His body language told me that he had decided that the door was no exit and the window was the only option, but he remembered that we were high up on the second floor. Before he could make an assault on the barrier of Holmes and myself and a dash into the room, I had moved forwards towards him to further limit the space he was confined to. He realised that he was a caged animal and shouted out to Miss Sutherland: 'I never wished to hurt you!' She was silent and deadly as she belted the riding crop down upon the side of his face with a crack! He reeled back, screaming in agony, clasping his cheek with one hand and holding up the other in an entreaty to his stepdaughter for mercy, but Miss Sutherland took no notice. She advanced two steps into the room and brought the crop down hard onto his shoulder, knocking him down onto the floor with its force. My word, these fat people had the advantage of sheer power from their volume! The scoundrel crawled around and moaned, like the coward he was, but Miss Sutherland gave no quarter and laid into him with three or four brutal lashes more before she stood back, hands on hips, breathing hard, and looked down upon him.

'Gentlemen!' she declared. 'Do we agree that this offal is beyond the law?'

*Mr. Windy-Pants deserved nothing less than a
darned good thrashing*

'Yes,' said Holmes. 'We can prove absolutely nothing. There is no point in alerting Scotland Yard. Watson?'

'The only punishment he will receive is that which you have administered already, Miss Sutherland. And a jolly fine show it was too.'

'It isn't over yet,' she cried. 'DE-BAG HIM!'

* * *

It was an hour later when the great detective threw himself down into his chair whilst laughing contentedly at the outcome of this most recent case. 'That fellow will rise from crime to crime until he does something very bad and ends up on the gallows.'

'First off, he will have to recover from the thrashing he has been given and buy some new trousers.'

We laughed together. 'Indeed! The fellow will not be able to sit down for a week after such a hiding!'

'And having those two constables waiting around the corner to arrest him for public indecency was a master-stroke. Well done!'

'These are the just desserts, but the case has, in some respects, been not entirely devoid of interest.'

'I cannot now entirely see all the steps of your reasoning,' I remarked.

'Of course, it was obvious from the first that this Mr. Hosmer Angel must have some strong object for his curious conduct, and it was equally clear that the only man who really profited by the incident, as far as we could see, was the stepfather. Then the fact that the two men were never together, but that the one always appeared when the other was away, was suggestive. So were the tinted spectacles and the curious voice, which both hinted at a disguise.'

'The hint was in the tint!' I quipped.

'Shut up, Watson, and listen...'

'DON'T you speak to John like that!' cried Rachel. I forgot to mention the unanticipated, unexpected, unannounced, but not unwelcome, arrival of Rachel Holmes to 221 Baker Street, just as Mr. Windibank was careering down the staircase on his escape to temporary freedom, his lower body all naked and bleeding.

'Well, *John*, my suspicions were all confirmed by his peculiar action in typewriting his signature, which of course inferred that his handwriting was so familiar to her that she would recognise even the smallest sample of it. You see all these isolated facts, together with many minor ones, all pointed in the same direction.'

'And how did you verify them *Sherlock*?' I asked.

'Having once spotted my man, it was easy to get corroboration. I knew the firm for which this man worked. Having taken the printed description, I eliminated everything from it which could be the result of a disguise – the whiskers, the glasses, the voice, and I sent it to the firm, with a request that they would inform me whether it answered the description of any of their travellers. I had already noticed the peculiarities of the typewriter, and I wrote to the man himself at his business address, asking him if he would come here. As I expected, his reply was typewritten, and revealed the same trivial but characteristic defects. The same post brought me a letter from Westhouse & Marbank, of Fenchurch Street, to say that the description tallied in every respect with that of the employee, James Windibank. *Voilà tout!*'

'I salute you, dear Brother,' said Rachel, 'because you have reasoned using the very latest technology and made the evidence into a perfectly accurate deduction. I am proud of you!'

'And what about Miss Sutherland?'

'You have no problem there,' she continued. 'In my short lifetime, I have encountered a woman as agitated as her before but never seen one so satisfied. Strange!'

'But how, *Sherlock*, did you include her in the final act to be played out in this very apartment?'

'I met with her at five o'clock, just before you returned here this evening from your day surgery. I gave her some of the bare facts and then positioned her in the room next to this.'

'You placed her in *my* bedroom?'

'Yes... John...in *your* bedroom. Then she was able to listen in on every word of our conversation with that scoundrel.'

'I would like to see your bedroom' said Rachel.

Holmes sprang up from his chair and looked down on us seated from his great loftiness. 'Certainly not! It is my duty to protect your reputation, Sister dear! You cannot enter a man's bedroom as a spinster. It will not do!'

Rachel's eyes widened, and then she stood up. "I will see John's bedroom! There is nothing untoward.' She grabbed me my by the shoulder, encouraging me to stand up as well. 'Sherlock, you are here to chaperone me. So is your housekeeper...?'

'Not Mrs. Hudson?' I shouted in trepidation, because, as you know, dear reader, Mrs. Hudson and I have a rather special relationship and I did not wish to alert her to my new friendship with Rachel.

'Yes... Mrs. Hudson is here, somewhere. In these circumstances, what could possibly impugn a reputation by looking into an unoccupied bedroom?'

'Ah! You may remember the old Persian saying?' said Holmes. '"He who peers through thy neighbour's window may see sights to offend his eye, and danger lies for whosoever snatches this illusion from a woman."'

'No,' said Rachel. 'I have never heard of it. And I do not see the relevance.'

She marched me out of the room, into the passage and then my bedroom, with Holmes in close pursuit. I turned up the light and, there, to my surprise and horror, was a disarray of untidiness: the blankets were in a tumble, half on the floor, the pillows were squashed and piled up, and the sheets looked like they had been ripped from the mattress by a bad-tempered gorilla. And there was a very strange smell about the place. Rachel pinched her nose and let out a squeak at the horrible sight.

'I don't live like this!' I had to say. 'I am at a loss about how to explain this turmoil! For some reason, unknown to me, Mrs. Hudson has not carried out her duties today.'

And then I remembered that she had! She was making up the bedrooms whilst Holmes and I had been taking breakfast that morning. As Rachel continued to study the mess, with an added "even the leg is broken!" remark, it dawned on me what had taken place that afternoon, in my room, and, in my bed. In the pregnant silence I turned around slowly to look at the culprit standing right behind me. His face was all mangled into an expression of guilt and smugness, worse than a hangman's career, and one that confessed to me, without a shred of doubt, that he had spent himself wickedly with Miss Sutherland that afternoon. There was the reason for her satisfied appearance of earlier. I walked up close to him, so that Rachel was out of earshot, and whispered.

'You will be clearing up this mess, Holmes, *and* you will be paying for our dinner!' I turned to Rachel. 'I have a table at the remarkable Rules, in Covent Garden. I will be honoured if you would join me?'

And, with that final word I put Rachel's hand in mine, and we marched past the despicable detective and out of the apartment, our heads held high in pious righteousness.

* * *